THIS WALKER BOOK BELONGS TO:

_____

_____

_____

For my dearest Rikka

First published 1992 by Walker Books Ltd
87 Vauxhall Walk, London SE11 5HJ

This edition published 2004

13 15 17 19 20 18 16 14 12

© 1992 Jez Alborough

The right of Jez Alborough to be identified as author/illustrator
of this work has been asserted by him in accordance with the
Copyright, Designs and Patents Act 1988

This book has been typeset in Garamond

Printed in China

British Library Cataloguing in Publication Data:
a catalogue record for this book
is available from the British Library

ISBN 978-1-84428-481-8

www.walker.co.uk

WHERE'S MY TEDDY?

JEZ ALBOROUGH

WALKER BOOKS
AND SUBSIDIARIES
LONDON • BOSTON • SYDNEY • AUCKLAND

Eddy's off to find his teddy.
Eddy's teddy's name is Freddy.

He lost him in the wood somewhere.
It's dark and horrible in there.

"Help!" said Eddy. "I'm scared already!
I want my bed! I want my teddy!"

He tip-toed
on and on
until …

something
made him stop
quite still.

Look out! he thought. There's something there!

WHAT'S THAT?

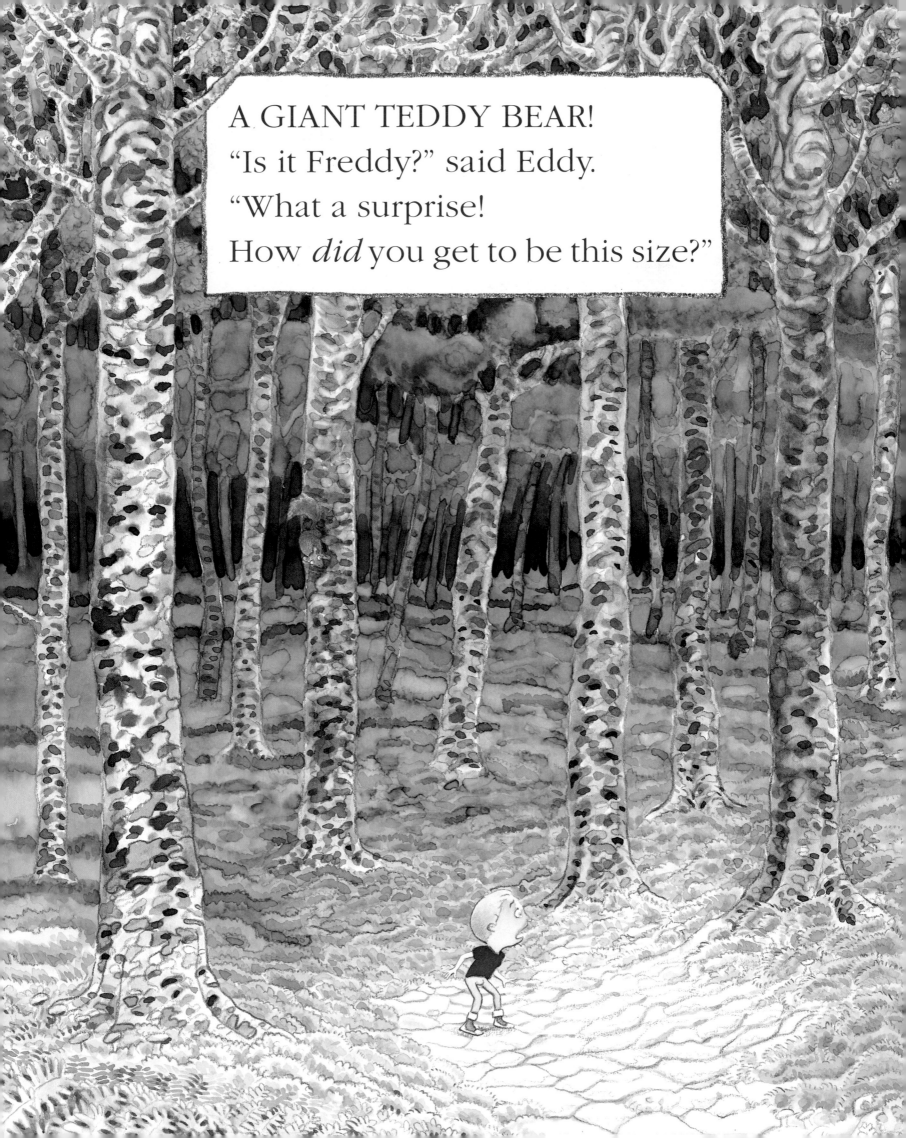

A GIANT TEDDY BEAR!
"Is it Freddy?" said Eddy.
"What a surprise!
How *did* you get to be this size?"

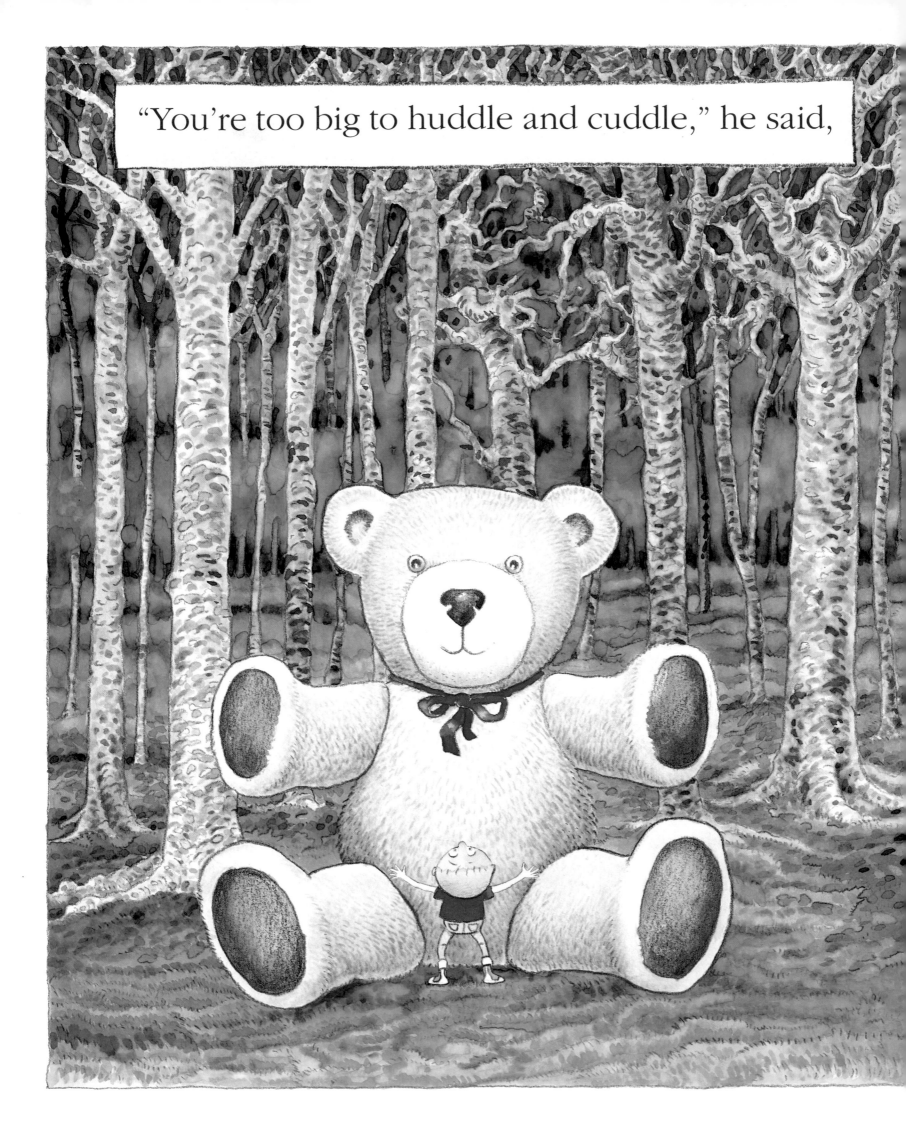

"You're too big to huddle and cuddle," he said,

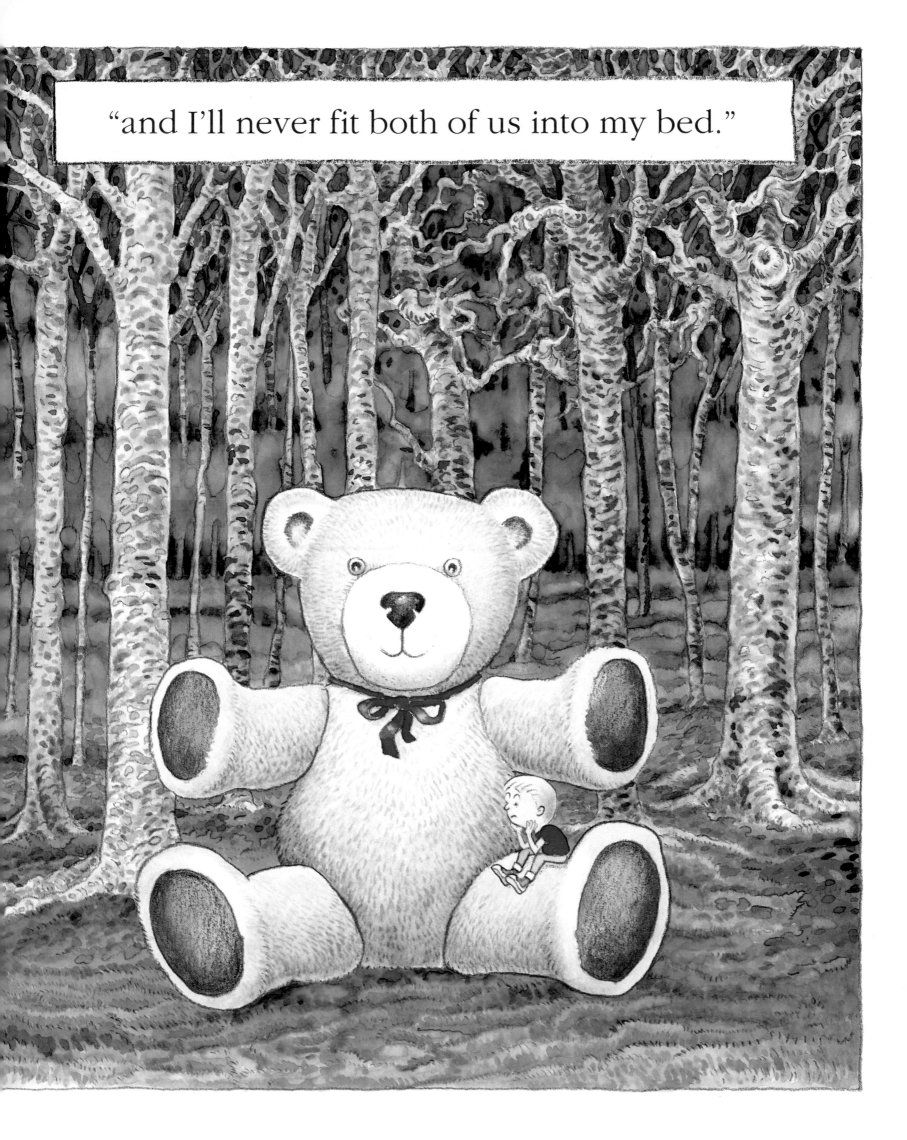

"and I'll never fit both of us into my bed."

Then out of the darkness,
clearer and clearer,
the sound of a sobbing
came nearer and nearer.

Soon the whole wood
could hear the voice bawl,
"How did you get to be
tiddly and small?
You're too small to
huddle and cuddle," it said,
"and you'll only get lost
in my giant-sized bed!"

It was a gigantic bear
and a tiddly teddy
stomping towards …

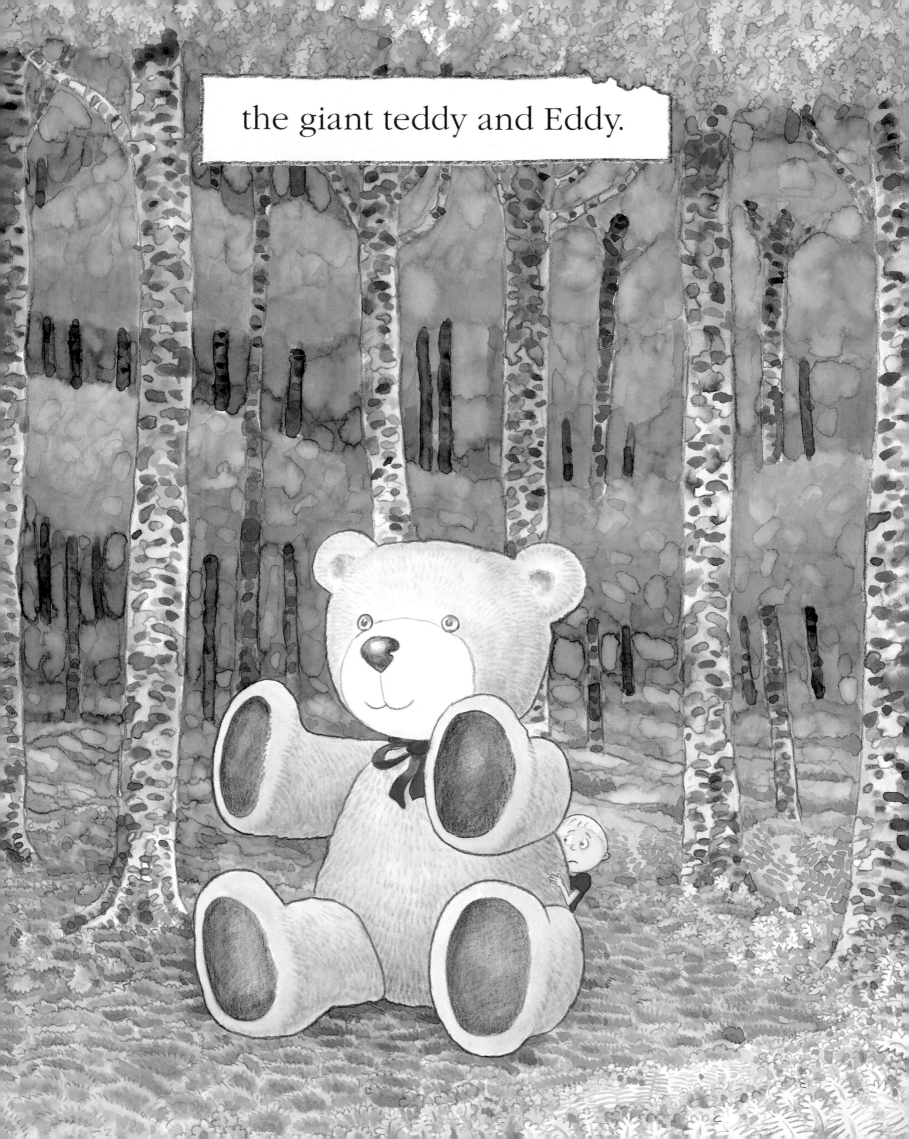

the giant teddy and Eddy.

"MY TED!"
gasped the bear.
"A BEAR!"
screamed Eddy.

"A BOY!"
yelled the bear.
"MY TEDDY!"
cried Eddy.

Then they ran and they ran
through the dark wood
back to their homes
as quick as they could ...

all the way back
to their snuggly beds,
where they huddled
and cuddled their
own little teds.

WALKER BOOKS is the world's leading
independent publisher of children's books.
Working with the best authors and illustrators
we create books for all ages, from babies
to teenagers – books your child will
grow up with and always remember. So…

FOR THE BEST CHILDREN'S BOOKS,
LOOK FOR THE BEAR